P9-CCW-260

Judy Moody

In a Monday Mood

Judy Moody

In a Monday Mood

Megan McDonald

illustrated by

Peter H. Reynolds

CANDLEWICK PRESS

First edition 2021

Library of Congress Catalog Card Number pending
ISBN 978-1-5362-1391-1

21 22 23 24 25 26 LBM 10 9 8 7 6 5 4 3 2 1

Printed in Melrose Park, IL, USA

This book was typeset in Stone Informal and Judy Moody.
The illustrations were done in watercolor, tea, and ink.

Candlewick Press
99 Dover Street
Somerville, Massachusetts 02144

www.candlewick.com

In memory of Cameron Boyce
MM and PHR

OCTOBER
29
NATIONAL
DAY

Table of Contents

Cats Bandicoot,
Zucchini Ninja

Creative genius with zucchini

Cocreator of
Blah Blah Blah Day

Stinkypants Poopstocking,
Zucchini Ninja partner
in crime

Who's Who

Mr. Bubble Wrap

Bubble Wrap popper

Human corn on the cob

Green-pancake eater

Pancakes Are for Saturdays

When she woke up on Monday morning, she, Judy Moody, had the blues. The Monday morning blues. The Monday morning blahs. Another week of school. Another week of spelling. Another week of Grouchy pencils.

Mondays were like a punch in the arm. Mondays were like a kick in the pants.

Crumbs! Why can't every day be Saturday? Judy wondered.

Stink could see that Judy was in a mood. "What's wrong?" he asked.

Judy twisted the curl on top of her head. "What's wrong? It's Monday, that's what."

"What's wrong with Monday?" Stink asked.

"It's not Saturday, that's what," said Judy.

Scritch-scratch. Stink scratched his head, thinking about that one.

"Name one good thing about Monday," Judy said.

Scritch-scratch. Stink scratched his head some more. "All the holidays fall on Mondays. You know, like Labor Day, and . . . and . . . a bunch of other days."

“That’s just it,” said Judy. “There are no Monday holidays coming up. There are no days off—no free days, teacher days, snow days. Nothing to look forward to.”

“C’mon. Let’s go eat breakfast. Maybe there will be silver-dollar pancakes. That’s something to look forward to.”

“Hello. It’s *Monday*, Stink. Dad never makes pancakes on Monday. Pancakes are for Saturdays.”

Downstairs, in the kitchen, Dad was flipping something at the stove. "Grab a plate," said Dad. "I made pancakes!"

"See?" said Stink. "Pancakes! And it's not even Saturday."

Dad plopped something on Judy's plate. Something round. Something *green*. Judy made a face.

"They're *zucchini* pancakes," said Dad.

"Green pancakes?" said Judy. "This day just keeps getting worse."

"Somebody has a bad case of the Mondays," said Mom.

"That would be Judy!" said Stink, pointing to his sister. He held his plate out, and Dad plopped a green pancake on it. "Pass the syrup, please."

P
S

"Mondays are the worst," said Judy.

"Good news," said Stink. "If you don't like Monday, it will be over in twenty-four hours."

"Let's see if I can help cheer you up," said Mom. She held up the spatula like a microphone. Dad held up the syrup bottle like a microphone. They put their heads together. They started singing!

They started singing an oldie kind of song, "Monday, Monday." They sang it at the top of their lungs.

Judy closed her eyes and covered her ears.

"Well, you can't say I didn't try," said Mom.

"C'mon, kids," said Dad. "Run up and get your backpacks. I'll walk you to the bus stop today."

"Stink," said Judy. "Can you grab my backpack? And make sure my spelling words are in there. And put some Grouchy pencils in the front pocket, too."

"Me?" said Stink. "Why can't you?"

"Because today's a special day after all," said Judy.

"It is?"

"It's National Do a Grouch a Favor Monday."

The Sound of Science

On Monday morning, Judy rode the same old bus to school. At school, she hung up her same old backpack in her same old orange locker. Then she slid into the same old seat at the same old desk behind Rocky.

She, Judy Moody, was feeling Monday-morning mopey. As dopey as a sloth.

"Same-same-same-same-same," Judy muttered to nobody in particular.

She looked around the room. There was the Doodle Board, the Positive Behavior Jar, the Writing Center. Same as every Monday.

Then, all of a sudden, she faced front and spied something *not* the same. Something different.

"Wait a minute," said super-sleuth Judy. Mr. Todd always had a bulletin board up front that said TOGETHER WE MAKE A RAINBOW. Everybody in Class 3T had a colorful paper crayon with his or her name on it.

It had been there on Friday, same as always. But now it was Monday, and the crayons were G-O-N-E *gone*. Instead of crayons, the board was covered with

animals. Sheep and fish and dragons made of Bubble Wrap.

Judy brightened a bit. A Monday mystery!

"Guys!" she said to Rocky and Frank. "Check it out." She pointed to the new bulletin board.

"What happened to the crayons with our names?" asked Rocky.

"Maybe the crayons quit," said Jessica. "Like in that book."

"But how will we know we are colorful and unique?" said Frank.

Just then, Mr. Todd blinked the lights. "Good morning, Class 3T!" he said brightly. "Are you ready for a *poppin'* good time?"

Jessica's hand shot up. "Is it a pop quiz? I hope it's a pop quiz."

The rest of Class 3T groaned.

"I hate to *burst your bubble,"* said Mr. Todd, "but it's

not a pop quiz." He laughed like he had told himself a joke. "It's much better than a pop quiz. Today is Monday, right?"

"Monday. Uggo," Judy muttered to herself.

"But it's not just any old Monday."

Not-uggo! Judy perked up.

"Today is a special day. A holiday, if you will."

Judy put on her best listening ears. She leaned forward, on the edge of her seat.

Mr. Todd reached into his book bag and pulled out a page-a-day calendar. He pointed to a page in January. Then he turned his back to the class. He was putting on a different tie. "Usually this holiday is celebrated on the last Monday in

January. But I thought we'd have a mix-it-up Monday. Who can wait till January? Am I right?"

He turned back around. "Ta-da! Today is . . . BUBBLE WRAP APPRECIATION DAY!" Mr. Todd hung up a Bubble Wrap curtain in the doorway. He set a Bubble Wrap sculpture of an elephant on his desk. Mr. Todd adjusted his tie. His tie was made out of Bubble Wrap!

Pop! Pop! Pop-pop-pop! Mr. Todd popped some Bubble Wrap bubbles. He pointed to the new bulletin board. "How do you like my *pop* art?"

Snap, crackle, and pop! Judy was cuckoo for Bubble Wrap. This boring old Monday just got a little less boring! RARE!

"Now, let's learn about Bubble Wrap." Mr. Todd held up a large piece. "What is Bubble Wrap used for?"

"You wrap it around stuff so it won't break," Hunter said.

"Exactly," said Mr. Todd. "But it didn't start out that way. Can you believe Bubble Wrap started out as wallpaper?"

"No way!"

"Wha?"

"Huh?"

"In nineteen fifty-seven, a pair of engineers set out to make cool wallpaper that had some kind of texture to it. They took two shower curtains and heat-sealed them together. But it had too many air bubbles trapped inside, and didn't work for wallpaper."

"I'd like that in my room," said Frank. "I could bounce off the walls. Kapow! Bam! Zam!"

"But they didn't give up. They made a list of four hundred things they could do with the plastic sheets. About a year later, one of those ideas caught on. They used it in packages as padding to keep things like computers from breaking. That's how Bubble Wrap was invented."

"Cool beans!" said Judy.

"Neato kabeeto!" said Hunter.

"Class 3T," said Mr. Todd, "imagine you are the inventors of Bubble Wrap. What are some ideas for how you might you use Bubble Wrap?"

"A bike helmet," said Hunter.

"A soccer ball," said Jessica Finch.

"Snow shoes, you know, to keep your feet warm," said Frank.

Judy had an idea. "How about a Bubble Wrap burglar alarm!"

"Hmm," said Mr. Todd. "How would that work?"

"Put Bubble Wrap inside the door. If a burglar breaks in and steps on it, you'd hear *pop-pop-pop-pop-pop*!"

"These are all good ideas," said Mr. Todd. "Who wants to hear about a pumpkin named Gourdzilla that weighed eight hundred and fifteen pounds?"

Every hand went up. "The company that makes Bubble Wrap once entered a pumpkin-dropping contest. They dropped a giant pumpkin from a thirty-five-foot-high crane onto layers of Bubble Wrap."

Splat! Squish! Squoosh! Class 3T made pumpkin-squishing sounds.

"I bet pumpkin guts got all over everything and everybody," said Hunter.

"The pumpkin didn't even break," said Mr. Todd. "It bounced!" He took out an egg carton and started passing out raw eggs.

“What are these for?” asked Jessica.

“Eggzilla!” said Judy.

“Judy’s right,” said Mr. Todd. “Everybody wrap your egg in Bubble Wrap and tape it so it won’t fall out. We’re going to conduct our very own Class 3T Egg Drop.”

One by one, Class 3T dropped eggs all over the classroom.

“Uh-oh, bubble trouble,” said Judy. “Mine cracked.”

“Is this how you make egg drop soup?” asked Hunter.

“Wow! Mine doesn’t have a scratch!” said Jessica Finch.

When the Eggzilla experiments were over, it was time. Time to pop!

SPLAT!

Mr. Todd passed out more sheets of Bubble Wrap. "I know Mondays can be stressful for some of us. Popping Bubble Wrap is fun, and it also helps with stress. On the count of three," said Mr. Todd. "One, two, three . . ."

Pop-pop-pop-pop-pop-pop-pop-pop-pop-pop-pop!

The whole classroom exploded with pops. It sounded like firecrackers. Ms. Tuxedo, the principal, came rushing

through the door. "What's going on in here?"

"It's the sound of science!" said Judy.

Class 3T explained all about Bubble Wrap Appreciation Day. And before you could say Eggzilla, the principal was popping bubbles and laughing, too.

"Mr. Todd says it helps with stress," Judy told the principal.

"That's good because I've had a stressful Monday," said Ms. Tuxedo.

Class 3T popped bubbles until they were too pooped to pop. Who knew a boring old punch-in-the-arm Monday could turn out to be such a special day?

Mr. Todd, World's Best Teacher, had turned Judy's Monday frown upside down. And if a Monday could be special, why not Tuesday, Wednesday, Thursday, and Friday?

The light bulb in Judy's brain switched on.

She, Judy Moody, had an Eggzilla of an idea. And it just-might-maybe hatch into a plan.

Ding-Dong Ditch

On Monday night, over green pizza (aka zucchini), Judy told her family all about Bubble Wrap Appreciation Day. She was popping with excitement. "Mr. Todd gave me a great idea! I'm going to make up a holiday to celebrate *every* day of the week. Not just Monday."

"Like what?" asked Stink.

"Stink, you wouldn't believe all the

wacky holidays we didn't even know about! Mr. Todd has a calendar that shows a crazy holiday for every day of the year. National Rubber Eraser Day. National No Socks Day. National Tell a Lie Day. No lie!"

"Is there a National Get Hit by an Asteroid Day? National Pluto Is a Planet Day? National Leave Poop on the Moon Day? The Apollo astronauts left ninety-six bags of poop on the moon. They should have a special day for that."

"I don't think there's a day for *that*, Stink. But there's probably a day for . . ." Judy looked around the kitchen. "Zucchini."

"Zucchini? Who would be wacky

enough to celebrate a big, giant green vegetable?"

"Let's find out," said Judy. Dinner was over, so they ran to the computer. Judy typed in Z-U-C-I-N-I.

Did you mean zucchini?

"Look," said Judy. "The computer even spelled it for me."

"Whoa," said Stink, peering at the screen. "The world's heaviest zucchini weighed sixty-five pounds. It weighed more than I do!"

"Yeah, but you're a shrimp-o," said Judy.

"No," said Stink. "I'm just height challenged." Judy cracked up.

"Let's see if there's any holidays—hey, guess what!" said Judy. "There's a National Sneak Some Zucchini onto Your Neighbor's Porch Day."

"What?" said Stink. He peered at the computer.

"It says so in the *Old Farmer's Almanac,*" said Judy. "See? It says to wait until the dead of night. Creep up to your neighbor's front door. Leave zucchini for them to enjoy."

"It also says that zucchini is a fruit, not a vegetable," said Stink. "Everybody likes fruit."

"Are you thinking what I'm thinking?" asked Judy.

Stink nodded. "Let's do it."

“Stink, you have ESP. You read my mind. Let’s go ask Dad.”

They ran back to the kitchen. Dad had a zucchini in a machine, and he was turning the handle.

“Dad? What are you making?” asked Stink. “A green volcano?”

“I’m making zoodles!” said Dad.

"Zucchini noodles. For dinner tomorrow. Grandma Lou still has zucchini in her garden, and she dropped off tons of them. I have zukes coming out of my ears."

"You do?" Stink pretended to look for zucchini in Dad's ears. "All I see is hair."

"Dad," said Judy. "What if we took care of all the zucchini for you?"

"Is this for an operation?" asked Dad. "Even Judy Moody, M.D., could not operate on all these zucchini."

"It's not for an operation," said Stink.

"Yes it is," said Judy. "It's for Operation Sneaky Zucchini!"

As soon as Dad gave the A-OK to give zucchini to their friends, Judy sprang into action. She tied bunches of zucchini together with ribbons and wrote funny notes to go with them. Then she and Stink loaded them into their backpacks.

"Wear dark clothes," said Judy, "so we can be ninjas and nobody will know it's us. And bring a flashlight."

"I'll wear my superhero eye mask," said Stink.

"Good idea," said Judy. "I'll wear my cat eye mask."

Judy imagined herself a nimble cat. She slunk down the sidewalk, trying not to make a sound. Stink tiptoed down the sidewalk with superhero invisibility.

"Let's hit Rocky's house first," said Judy. "It's the closest."

"Our neighbors will get a trick *and* a treat from us," said Stink. "And it's not even Halloween!"

When they got to Rocky's house, they ducked behind a bush. Stink unzipped his backpack. Judy put her finger to her lips. "Tell your zipper to be quieter," she whispered.

Stink took a bundle of zucchini from his backpack.

"Remember, Stink," said Judy. "The

plan is Ding-Dong Ditch! You put the zucchini outside the door. I'll ring the bell. Then we run like the wind."

"Ding-Dong Ditch," said Stink. "Got it."

They crept up the front steps. Stink set the zucchini on the welcome mat. Judy pressed the bell and . . . ran.

They ducked behind some bushes in Rocky's front yard. Dogs barked from the house next door. Judy peered through the leaves. Rocky answered the door. He looked all around. He saw the zucchini. He picked it up. He read the note.

Dear Rocky, You're a magician. Make these disappear.

"Who's at the door, Rocky?" his mom called.

"Nobody," said Rocky. "Just some cucumbers."

Judy covered her mouth and cracked up. Stink laughed so hard, he had to try not to shake the bushes.

"Who's next?" Stink asked when Rocky had gone back inside.

"Jessica Finch!" said Judy.

The Zucchini Ninjas sneak-snuck-slunk all over the neighborhood, delivering random acts of zucchini. When they rang Jessica Finch's bell, she opened the door and read the note:

Pop quiz. What am I?

a) a vegetable

b) a fruit

c) a squash

d) all of the above

PeeGee WeeGee, her pet pig, went crazy. He snorted and oinked and ran in circles.

"Since when do you like zucchini?" they heard Jessica ask him. "Or pop quizzes?"

"Let's go to Izzy's next," said Judy. "She lives at her dad's house now."

When Izzy Azumi opened the door and saw the zucchini, she screamed. "Dad! We have a burglar! A zucchini burglar."

Judy held her breath.

Izzy's brother came running to the door. He picked up the zucchini with the note. "It's not a burglar," he said. "A burglar steals. A burglar doesn't give you stuff. Or leave a note."

"A note! What's it say?" asked Izzy.

Her brother read the note aloud. *"What did the pumpkin say to the zucchini?"* Izzy shrugged. *"Stop being green with envy."*

"At least it's a funny burglar," said Izzy.

Izzy's dad came up behind them. "I wonder who left us these beautiful zucchini?" he said. "I can make zucchini bread. Or zucchini *pancakes*. C'mon inside, kids." He shut the door.

Judy let out her breath. "Poor Izzy," said Judy. "Now she has to eat green pancakes."

Stink grinned.

"We have one bundle left," said Stink. "Who's it for?"

"Nobody," said Judy. "I'm all out of notes."

"How about we take it to Frank Pearl?"

"Too far," said Judy. "Dad said we have to stay where he can see us from the porch."

On their way back home, they paused in front of Mrs. Soso's house, right next door to their own. Stink looked at Judy. Judy looked at Stink.

"Are you thinking what I'm thinking?" Stink asked.

"One last Ding-Dong Ditch!" said Judy.

Professor Carrot

The next day at the bus stop, everybody was talking about the Zucchini Ninja.

"The doorbell rang, and there was nobody there but cucumbers!" said Rocky.

"You mean zucchini," said Jessica.

"Same here!" said Izzy.

"Freaky-deaky," said Stink, trying to fake them out. Judy gave him a thumbs-up. "Did anybody besides Izzy have to eat green pancakes for breakfast?"

Judy gave Stink the hairy eyeball.

"How did you know?" Izzy asked.

Rocky looked at Judy. Judy stared at the ground. "Wait a minute," said Rocky. "This smells like a Judy Moody idea."

Judy couldn't help it. She burst out laughing.

"It *was* you!" said Rocky, pointing at Judy.

"It was *you*?" said Jessica and Izzy at the same time.

"Gotcha!" Judy cried. "I got you guys so good."

"Don't forget me," said Stink, pointing to himself. "I was a Zucchini Ninja, too!"

Judy explained all about mopey Mondays. "Mr. Todd started it with Bubble

Wrap Appreciation Day yesterday. I got the idea to make every day a holiday this week. Then Stink and I read about Sneak Some Zucchini onto Your Neighbor's Porch Day last night."

"No way is that a real thing," Rocky said.

"*The Old Farmer's Almanac* does not lie," said Judy.

"You guys sure were sneaky," said Rocky. "I didn't see you at all."

"PeeGee WeeGee went crazy!" said Jessica. "I'm sure he thought it was a dog."

"I thought I heard a burglar," said Izzy. "A zucchini burglar!"

"Happy National Sneak Some Zucchini

onto Your Neighbor's Porch Day!" said Judy.

"What is today's holiday going to be?" asked Jessica.

"Okay. I was thinking. Instead of National Dress Up Your Pet Day or National Eat Your Vegetables Day, we could have National Dress Up a Vegetable Day," said Judy. "Party at my house after school. And don't forget your veggies."

Judy thought she heard Jessica say something about corn on the cob, but she couldn't be sure. She was already half-way up the bus steps.

At school that day, Judy still had zucchini on the brain. In math class, she made up a problem using fractions.

If your dog eats one quarter of a zucchini, how much of the zucchini is left? In Spanish, Judy learned the Spanish word for zucchini. *El calabacín.* And in Spelling, when Mr. Todd asked her to spell *graffiti*, Judy spelled Z-U-C-C-H-I-N-I.

"Even though that's not one of our spelling words today," said Mr. Todd, "I'm impressed that you spelled it correctly."

After school, Judy and Stink ran home from the bus stop to get ready for Dress Up a Vegetable Day. When Judy got to the front door, she stopped. Somebody had left a whole basket of veggies on the front steps.

"Check it out, Stink. We got veggied!"

"Maybe today is Sneak Eggplants, Squash, and Peppers onto Your Neighbor's Porch Day."

Judy read the note. "It's from Mrs. Soso. To thank us for the zucchini."

Stink's eyes got wide. "How did she know it was us? We were so ninja."

Judy shrugged.

Stink groaned. "So now we have to eat even more veggies?"

"I have a better idea," said Judy. "We can use them for Dress Up a Vegetable Day instead. Perfect timing!"

Judy spread out art supplies all over the floor. Tape and glue and markers. Yarn and felt and Bubble Wrap and googly eyes. "There. Everybody can use art supplies to decorate a vegetable. Then we can have a parade or something for Dress Up a Vegetable Day. What do you think?"

“March of the Vegetables! I like it. I’m going to make a vegetable into a superhero. I’ll dress up a carrot with a mask and cape. Professor Carrot by day, Carrot Cake Crusader by night.”

The doorbell rang. “I’ll get it!” Judy ran to answer the door.

Rat Stew and Pizza Soup

When Judy opened the door, there stood a four-foot, one-inch corn on the cob!

She stared, her mouth half-open.

"It's me! Jessica!" said Jessica Finch.

"I know, but . . ." said Judy. "You're corn on the cob! Why are you wearing your costume from when we ran the Turkey Trot?"

Just then, a carrot and an eggplant came waltzing up the sidewalk.

"How do you like my eggplant?" asked Izzy, twirling around in a circle.

Rocky was dressed in bright orange pants and an orange T-shirt. His hat looked like a carrot top. "This is from when I was an orange sea cucumber in the school play *Under the Sea*. It's the best I could do on short notice."

Judy just stared some more.

"Why aren't you saying anything?" asked Jessica.

"I don't get it," said Judy. "Why are you all dressed like vegetables?"

"You said it was Dress Up Like a Vegetable Day," said Izzy.

Jessica the corncob nodded. "You told us to come over to celebrate."

"Let's get this party started," said Rocky the carrot.

Judy couldn't help laughing her pants off. "I said it was Dress Up a Vegetable Day," said Judy. "Not Dress Up *as* a Vegetable Day!"

"You mean I wore all this orange for nothing?" Rocky asked. "I walked down the street looking like a giant carrot!"

"Good thing you didn't get attacked by a giant rabbit!" said Judy. They all laughed even harder.

Judy led her friends into the family room. She pointed to the art supplies. "We were going to dress up vegetables to make them look funny. You know, like the Potato Head toys, or that talking broccoli."

"Oh, now I get it," said Rocky, smacking his forehead.

"Did anybody bring their zucchini?" Judy asked. Nobody had. "We can still decorate vegetables. Stink, go get the basket we got from Mrs. Soso, okay?"

Stink zoomed to the kitchen. When he came back, he had an uh-oh look on his face. "Bad news," said Stink.

"What's wrong?" asked Judy. "Where are the veggies?"

"Dad used them already."

"What for?" asked Judy.

"Dinner," said Stink. "And it's worse than green pancakes."

"What could be worse than green pancakes?" Judy asked. She hopped up and

went to the kitchen. The others followed. A big pot was boiling away on the stove.

"It *smells* good," said Judy.

"Trust me. It's not," said Stink.

"What is it?" Judy asked.

"Rat stew," said Stink.

"Aargh!" Judy stuck out her tongue. Rocky gagged. Jessica covered her mouth. Izzy made a face.

Dad came into the kitchen to check on his stew. "Hey, kids. What's up with the costumes? Is it Vegetable Awareness Day at school or something?"

"Or something," said Judy.

"I made stew. Anybody want to stay for dinner? You're all dressed for it," he said, chuckling.

"Noooo!" Everybody shrieked and backed away from the stew.

Dad offered Judy a spoonful. He blew on it. "Here. Take a taste."

"I know you like to cook weird stuff, Dad," said Judy, "but NO WAY am I eating rat stew."

"Rat stew!" said Dad. "Where did you get that idea?"

"Stink said that's what you called it."

"It's ratatouille," said Dad.

"Rat-ta-too-ee?" Judy asked.

"Yes, it's a French stew made of egg-plant, zucchini, peppers, and tomatoes."

"Eggplant. Yuck," said Stink.

"It's better than rats," said Judy. "I'll taste it." She slurped the stew right off the big spoon.

"What do you think?" asked Dad.

"It's yummy," said Judy. "Kind of like pizza soup."

"Pizza soup!" said Izzy. "I'm in!"

Dad passed out small bowls, and before you could say *rat-ta-too-ee*, everybody was slurping stew.

"Happy Rat Stew Day!" said Judy.

"What holiday is tomorrow going to be?" asked Izzy.

"I hope it has to do with magic," said Rocky. "Not zucchini."

"I'm hoping for pigs," said Jessica.

"How about dogs," said Izzy.

"Not even close," said Judy. "Tomorrow is . . . Wait. I'll show you." She got up from her chair, tucked her thumbs in her armpits, and flapped her arms in the air.

Stink raised his hand. "Is it National Act Like a Chicken Day?"

"National Walk Like a Duck Day?" asked Izzy.

"Nope!" said Judy. She started bobbing her head up and down.

"National Bob for Apples Day?" asked Jessica.

"No!" said Judy, laughing. "Tomorrow we're making bird feeders in art class. Tomorrow is Feed the Birds Day!"

Ninja Squirrel

The next day, when Class 3T got to the art room, long tables were littered with plastic bottles, cardboard tubes, milk cartons, cans, and craft sticks.

"Welcome, friends," said Ms. Ortiz. "Today we are going to make bird feeders out of recycled things. Then we'll go outside and hang them in the Peace Garden."

BIRD SEED
Sunflow
Butter

Class 3T rolled cardboard tubes in sunflower butter and birdseed. They built feeders out of craft sticks. They decorated bottles and clipped clothespins to cans for perches.

"Now we're ready to hang them up and watch for birds to come find our feeders," said Ms. Ortiz. "What kind of birds do you think we might be able to spot in our school garden?"

"Those red ones and the blue ones," said Frank Pearl.

"Cardinals and bluebirds, yes," said Ms. Ortiz.

"Finches!" said Jessica Finch.

"It would be way-cool to see a woodpecker," said Judy.

"We might see a hairy woodpecker," said Ms. Ortiz. "Or a red-headed woodpecker. Also sparrows, wrens, and chickadees."

Class 3T went outside to the Peace Garden. The garden had painted peace rocks, stepping stones made by students, and a friendship fountain. In the center was a peace pole that spelled *peace* in different languages.

Ms. Ortiz helped them hang their feeders from T-shaped poles. They strung a rope across the garden from tree to tree to hang the rest. Before they knew it, art class was over.

"But we didn't get to see any birds," said Hunter.

"It might take some time for the birds to discover your feeders."

All during Social Studies, Judy stared out the window. She thought she heard a *tap-tap-tap*ping. She craned her neck to see. No woodpecker in sight. Was that a whoosh of wings that went by? She stood up so she could see better.

"Judy Moody," said Mr. Todd. "You seem to be having trouble staying in your seat today. In fact, the whole class is looking out the window instead of learning about life in Alaska. What's going on?"

"It's the birds!" said Frank Pearl.

"We're watching for birds to come to the feeders we made in art class," said Jessica.

"Tell you what," said Mr. Todd. "Alaska can wait. Let's take an in-class mini field trip over to the window and see what we can observe in the garden."

Class 3T bounced out of their seats and over to the window.

"I see a rock!" said Bradley.

"I see a lizard!" said Hannah K. It darted under the rock.

"I see a black-and-blue butterfly," said Piper.

"It's called a pipevine swallowtail," said Mr. Todd.

"C'mon, birds," said Rocky, crossing his fingers.

"How can this be Feed the Birds Day if we don't feed any birds?" Judy asked. Just then, she heard a tiny call. *Fee-bee. Fee-bee.* A small black-capped chickadee

flew in and perched on one of the feeders.

"That's my feeder!" Rocky said, pointing.

The bird flitted and hopped from feeder to feeder.

Next a yellow finch flew in. And another.

"I see a finch," said Judy. "A not–Jessica Finch!" She cracked herself up.

For a few minutes, they stood at the window, rapt, watching the birds.

All of a sudden, Class 3T spotted a bushy-tailed intruder.

A beady-eyed squirrel made its way across the rope—upside down! It got close to one of the feeders, stretched itself out to reach it, and started munching.

"Hey, that squirrel's stealing all the birdseed!"

"What a sneak. That squirrel's some kind of ninja. Ninja Squirrel!"

"At least Ninja Squirrel can't climb up those metal poles to get to the other feeders."

Ninja Squirrel tried to run up one of the poles. The pole shook back and forth. *Boing!* The squirrel slid back down. It tried again. *BOING!* Ninja Squirrel slid down again. And again.

Then Ninja Squirrel did something super sneaky. Super

stealth. It darted over to the oak tree. It raced up the tree trunk. It scampered out to the tip of the branch.

WHEEE! Ninja Squirrel went flying—out of the tree and through the air. It landed with its front two feet on an empty arm of the pole. *Shoop. Shoop. Shoop.* The

squirrel spun around three times fast in a triple somersault before it stuck the landing.

Class 3T laughed. Class 3T clapped. Class 3T cheered.

"Whoa! Ninja Squirrel can do gymnastics!"

"Ninja Squirrel could win the Squirrel Olympics."

"Look," said Jessica Finch. "Now it's burying one of the nuts."

"Just think," said Mr. Todd. "A squirrel may have planted that big oak tree."

"Huh?" everybody asked.

"When a squirrel buries acorns, it usually forgets some of its hiding places, and a tree grows!"

"RARE!" said Judy.

"Some squirrels even *pretend* to bury a nut, to trick other squirrels that might try to steal nuts from them."

"That's like a Jedi mind trick!" said Hunter.

"How do they find the nuts they buried?" Judy asked.

"They use their sense of smell. Squirrels can smell nuts they buried even under a foot of snow."

Class 3T got carried away watching Ninja Squirrel zigzag around the garden, burying nuts. Soon they forgot all about the birds.

"Squirrels are super amazing!" said Hannah K.

"Especially ninja squirrels," said Hunter.

"Too bad about Feed the Birds Day," Rocky said to Judy.

"Happy Feed a Ninja Squirrel Day!" Judy said happily.

This week had started off with a bad-mood Monday. And now it had turned into a wowza Wednesday!

Cats Bandicoot and Stinkypants Poopstocking

When Judy woke up on Thursday, she pulled on her Screamin' Mimi's ice-cream socks. An idea popped into her head.

She hurried down to breakfast. The coast was clear—Mom and Dad were not in the kitchen. Judy poured herself a glass of orange juice. Then she plopped a spoonful of vanilla ice cream into her orange juice.

Stink bounded into the kitchen. He pointed at Judy. "Hey! You have a milk mustache! Is this National Wear a Milk Mustache Day or something?"

"Or something," said Judy. She wiped her mouth. "For your information, Stink, it's not a milk mustache. It's an *ice-cream* mustache."

"What?"

"Today is National Eat Ice Cream for Breakfast Day!"

Stink ran to the freezer. He plopped a spoonful of ice cream on his cereal.

Dad came in the back door, whistling. Mom set down Mouse the cat.

"Who left the ice cream out?" asked Dad.

"And *why* is the ice cream out at all?" Mom asked.

Judy slugged down the rest of her orange juice.

"It's National Eat Ice Cream for Breakfast Day!" Stink announced.

"*Secret* National Eat Ice Cream for Breakfast Day," Judy mumbled.

“Sorry,” said Mom. “No ice cream for breakfast.”

Just then, Judy burped. “Oops. Too late.”

“I think you better dream up a new holiday for today,” said Dad.

“How about National Talk Like a Pirate Day?” said Stink. “Aye, matey?”

“Shiver me timbers,” said Judy. “I’m already out of pirate sayings. How about National Flip-Flop Day?”

"You wear those every day," said Stink.

"How about National Brush Your Teeth and Get Ready for School Day?" said Mom.

"BOR-ing," said Judy.

"We do *that* every day," said Stink.

"I think Mom means it's time for school," said Dad.

"But we haven't figured out a special holiday for today," said Judy.

"You have all day to think about it," said Mom.

"Stink, you make a list and I'll make a list and we'll decide after school."

Stink pulled a pencil from behind his ear. "On it!"

@ @ @

At last! It was finally After-School Time. Judy and Stink stretched out on the floor of the family room. Stink read from his list.

"How about National Read the Encyclopedia Day?"

"You made that up. Let's hear some ideas that are real holidays."

"How about National Something on a Stick Day? It's for real. I looked it up. You know how I love foods that come on a stick."

"You have corn dogs on the brain," said Judy.

"Okay, then you go," said Stink.

Judy unfolded her list. "How about National Pencil Day?"

"You're the only one who's cuckoo for pencils," said Stink.

"National Thank a Mail Carrier Day? We could make thank-you cards and give them to Jack Frost for being such a good mailman."

"But the mail already came today," said Stink. "Next."

"Okay. Okay. How about National Tell a Lie Day?"

"I like your socks," said Stink.

Judy stuck out her foot to see. "You do?

"No. I lied."

"Well, I like your Food on a Stick idea," said Judy.

"You do?

"No, *I* lied," said Judy.

"Forget it," said Stink. "It's too hard to guess if you're lying." He looked at his list. "How about National Underwear Day? It's officially on August fifth. But who cares? We could try to break a record for the most people we can get to go outside wearing only underwear."

"So you're going to go outside in nothing but your tighty-whities?"

"I'll wear my superhero Spider-Man Underoos."

"Get real, Stink. I'm not going outside in my undies."

"Not even to thank a mail carrier?" asked Stink.

"Ha, ha," said Judy. "How about National Thrift Shop Day? We could ask Mom or Dad to take us."

"Nah. There's never anything good there," said Stink.

"Ya-huh. Last time I found a pencil box that looks like chocolate milk, a book of mini-mysteries, and a T-shirt so big it would fit a giant."

Stink was not convinced. They both looked at their lists again.

"National Save a Penny Day?" Stink asked.

"Veto!" said Judy, shaking her head no. "National Save the Honeybees Day?"

"Veto," said Stink. He ran out of good ideas on his list. Stink stuck his hand under the cushion on the couch. He came up with a bubble-gum wrapper, a rubber band, an old jelly bean, and lint. "National Search for a Jelly Bean Day?"

"Veto," said Judy. "National Get a Different Name Day? I can be Cats Bandicoot. You can be . . . Stinkypants Poopstocking."

"Thanks a lot." He made up a new idea. "National Raise My Allowance Day?"

"Mom and Dad will never go for that, Stink. Besides, making every day a holiday was my idea, so I should get to choose."

"You always get to choose!" said Stink, raising his voice. "And I'm not doing pencils!" He threw down his notebook.

"Hey! Hey! Hey!" said Mom and Dad, coming into the family room. "What is going on in here?"

"Ask Cats Bandicoot," said Stink, crossing his arms.

"Stink's being a baby. As usual," said Judy. "And it's not even National Act Like a Baby Day."

"Well National Name-Calling Day has to stop right now," said Dad.

"We're trying to come up with a special day for today and Judy won't let me do any of my ideas," said Stink.

"He doesn't like my ideas, either," said Judy.

"How about if Dad and I decide what special day this is going to be."

"Fine," said Judy.

"Fine," said Stink.

Mom and Dad whispered to each

other. Then Mom announced, "We declare today . . ."

Stink crossed his fingers. "Don't say pencil, don't say pencil."

"No underwear allowed," said Judy.

"National Get Along with Your Sibling Day!"

Judy scowled. Stink pouted. Judy frowned. Stink sulked. Judy wrinkled her brow. Stink sneered with one side of his nose. Judy made a face. Stink made a face.

All of a sudden, they both started laughing.

"That's better," said Mom and Dad.

"For the next half hour we want you to come up with something you can do *together* to show us that you can get along," said Mom.

"Pretend it's National Peace and Quiet Day," said Dad.

"I have an idea!" said Judy. "You're going to like my idea this time, Stink. I promise." She raced up the stairs. Stink ran after her. For the next half hour, the only sounds that could be heard from Judy's room were squeaky markers and laughter.

"We did a great job," said Judy, admiring their work. "Yay, us!"

"We had fun. *And* we got along," said Stink.

"Two heads *are* better than one," said Judy. They cracked themselves up.

"Siblings rule!" said Stink.

"Let's go celebrate Make Mom and Dad Happy Day." Judy scooped up their creation and crept silently down the stairs.

Judy and Stink slipped the giant T-shirt over their heads. They each poked one arm out of a sleeve, and both of their heads stuck out through the top.

On Judy's side, the shirt said:

MY BROTHER IS:

~~STINKY~~

SMART

FULL OF SCIENCE

On Stink's side, the shirt said:

MY SISTER IS:

~~MOODY~~

FUNNY

FULL OF IDEAS

Mom and Dad were sitting on the couch. Judy and Stink waddled into the family room.

"Happy National Get Along with Your Sibling Day!" they shouted.

MY BROTHER
IS
~~STINKY~~
SMART
FULL OF
SCIENCE
MY
SISTER
IS
~~MOODY~~
FUNNY
FULL
OF
IDEAS

Pet Rocks for Peace

The next day, Judy, Rocky, Stink, and Izzy stepped off the bus at the corner of Croaker Road. An old lady in a wide-brimmed purple hat sat on the opposite corner waving a peace flag.

"It must be Friday," said Judy, waving. "The Purple Hat Lady is on her corner."

"Who's the Purple Hat Lady?" asked Izzy Azumi.

"Every Friday, rain or shine, the Purple Hat Lady sits on the corner and people honk at her and wave."

They ran across the street to the opposite corner. "Hi! I'm Judy Moody," said Judy. "I live down the street and these are my friends. We were wondering why everybody honks at you."

The old lady smiled and flipped over a sign that said HONK IF YOU LIKE PEACE. "It's

my Wear Purple for Peace protest. I come here every Friday to remind people that we need peace. War is not the answer. We humans need to be kind to each other, don't you think? My hope is that we try to get along and work together to make the world a better place."

"I'm for peace," said Judy. "And I have lots of purple."

"Just yesterday my sister and I had to learn peace for thirty whole minutes," Stink told her.

Honk, honk!

"Good for you," said the Purple Hat Lady. "We all need to practice peace a little more."

"Great idea. I'm going to go put on

some purple and spread some more peace," said Judy. The old lady chuckled.

"It's official," said Judy. "Today is National Wear Purple for Peace Day!"

"Let's *all* go home and put on purple!" said Izzy.

"Okay. As long as you don't dress up like an eggplant," Judy teased.

"Meet back at Judy's house as soon as you can," Rocky called. "Tell everybody!"

Judy and Stink ran home. Judy rummaged through her closet. She came up with a purple tie-dye T-shirt and a purple beret. She drew peace signs on her purple high-top sneakers.

Stink was wearing a purple T-shirt, too. "Your shirt's on backward," said Judy.

Stink turned around slowly. His shirt said LITTLE MISS SECOND GRADE. Judy laughed out loud. "What are you wearing?"

"It's the only purple I could find. It belongs to Sophie of the Elves. She left it at karate the other day, and I didn't give it back to her yet."

"Here. Let me." Stink held his arms in the air, and Judy pulled off his shirt. She turned it inside out. Stink wriggled back into the shirt. "There. You're good to go."

Judy and Stink brought out face paint and craft paint and sidewalk chalk. Their friends were already outside, wearing purple.

"Happy Wear Purple for Peace Day!" said Izzy, grinning. She painted a peace sign on Judy's face. Judy painted a smiley eggplant on Izzy's cheek.

Rocky and Jessica Finch collected rocks. Stink drew peace signs with chalk on the sidewalk. Everybody painted rocks with suns and hearts and flowers and rainbows. They wrote words like *kind* and *joy* and *peace* and *calm* on the rocks.

"We could put these in the Peace Garden at school," said Jessica.

"They're like pet rocks, only for peace!" said Judy.

"Pet rocks for peace!" Stink yelled.

"Yelling isn't exactly peace, Stink," said Judy. "These rocks are supposed to help you feel peaceful when you hold them."

"When I hold mine," said Stink, "it makes me want to shout for peace." Stink waved a HONK FOR PEACE sign at anybody passing by. Mrs. Soso drove by and honked. Frank Pearl's mom dropped him off and tooted. Even Mr. Todd cruised by in his Mini. He beeped and waved.

Pretty soon, lots of friends and neighbors had joined in. Stink's friends Webster and Sophie of the Elves were painting peace rocks, too.

"Is that my shirt?" asked Sophie.

"Don't ask," said Stink.

All of a sudden, fourth-grade book whiz Mighty Fantaskey rode up on her bike. "Happy Wear Purple for Peace Day!" she called. "And it's not even May sixteenth!" She ran over to them. She was wearing alien deely boppers on her head, three-fingered gloves, and a shirt that said STAY WEIRD.

"Hi, Mighty!" Judy called.

"I couldn't wait to come over," said Mighty. "I love aliens!"

"I—I don't get it," said Judy. "What do aliens have to do with peace?"

"You know that Wear Purple for Peace Day is all about peace between earthlings and visitors from outer space, right?" said Mighty.

"It *is*?" asked Judy.

"It is?" asked Stink.

"It is?" asked Izzy and Rocky and Jessica.

"Yep. It sure is." Mighty held up three fingers. "Goony al peep!"

Judy looked confused. "What does that mean?"

"It means 'We come in peace' in Alien," said Mighty. Everybody burst out laughing.

Goony al peep!
STay a weird

"How do you say 'Happy Purple for Peace Day' in Alien?" Judy asked. "Goony al purpla?"

"No idea," said Mighty, laughing.

"This day just keeps getting weirder," said Stink.

"This day just keeps getting better," said Judy.

Blah Blah Blah Day

Judy slumped. Judy grumped. Even the curl on top of her head sagged. She, Judy Moody, was in a mood. She chewed the eraser on the end of her Grouchy pencil.

"How come you're in a mood?" asked Stink. "It's *Saturday*. You love *Saturday*. Isn't *Saturday* what you've been waiting for all week?"

"That's just it, Stink. Saturdays are already special. I have to think up an extra-special, super-duper genius idea for today."

"Mom and Dad to the rescue!" said Mom.

"Mom and I thought of the perfect holiday for a Saturday," said Dad. They held up a banner and unfolded it letter by letter.

Stink watched the letters *H-A-P-P-Y* unfold. The next letter was a *B*. "Happy

Birthday?" asked Stink. "Whose birthday is it?"

"Wait for it . . ." said Dad. The next letter after *B* was an *L*. Then *A*. Then *H*.

"Happy . . . Blah Day?" asked Judy.

They unfolded the banner to reveal all the letters.

"Ta-da!" said Mom. Judy read the banner.

"Happy *Blah Blah Blah* Day?" said Judy.

“That sounds fun,” said Stink.

“Unless it’s blah,” said Judy. “Then it’s no fun.”

"Now, officially this day is on April seventeenth,” said Mom, “but Dad and I thought it would be perfect for today.”

“What do you think?” asked Dad. “Are you in?”

Judy did not have a better idea. Stink nodded yes. “We’re in!”

“Great! Did you know that the words *blah blah blah* started back in ancient Greece?” said Dad. “It used to be *bar bar bar.*”

“Then it was *yada yada yada,*” said Mom.

“So this is a day where you and Dad

tell stories?" asked Stink.

"You know how when someone is talking, and all you hear is *blah blah blah*?" said Dad.

"Like right now?" asked Stink.

"Exactly!" said Judy. Dad couldn't help cracking a smile. Mom grinned, too.

"International Blah Blah Blah Day is when you finally listen to those voices that have been nagging you, telling you to do things you don't always feel like doing."

"It's a day to cross things off your to-do list. Like starting a piggy bank," said Mom.

"Or painting the ceiling. Or visiting your grandma," said Dad.

"Ooh. Can I have stars and planets on my ceiling?" asked Stink.

"So we're going to see Grandma Lou?" Judy asked.

"Those are just examples," said Dad. "First on the *real* to-do list for Blah Blah Blah Day is . . . we want you both to clean your rooms."

"Huh?" said Stink.

"Blah," said Judy. Suddenly, Saturday had just gotten a little more Monday.

"Are you sure this isn't National Trick Your Kids into Doing Chores Day?"

"Sorry, guys," said Dad. "But we've already decided."

"If you get your rooms cleaned up, we can have Family Game Night in the

*day*time," said Mom. "Before dinner."

"With popcorn?" asked Stink.

@ @ @

Judy and Stink trudged upstairs. Judy stared at the mess in her room.

Piles of pillows, heaps of toys, mountains of books, stashes of stuffed animals, doll parts, and pizza tables were everywhere. Her finger-knitting chain snaked its way all across her room.

"Who made such a mess in here, Mouse?" she asked.

Judy picked up her I ATE A SHARK shirt. She turned it right side out. She put it on. There! One less thing on the floor. She felt a little better already.

She tossed all of her stuffed animals

onto her top bunk and pulled the quilt over them. Hmm. Her bed looked extra lumpy. Would Mom and Dad notice?

Judy put all of her pizza tables in a shoebox. *How many were in her collection?* She dumped them back out and decided to count them. Thirty-six pizza tables. RARE!

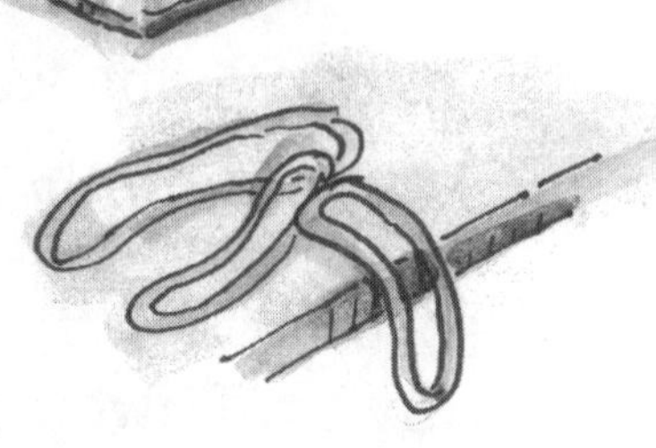

Judy lifted Jaws, her Venus flytrap, and found her Mood Libs. She sat down and filled in a place, a color, an animal, until it sounded super silly. Then she read it aloud to Mouse.

Judy picked up her tiger-striped pajamas. There was her loom, with tons of cotton loops. Time to make a pot holder!

Under her Hedda-Get-Betta doll was Nancy Drew Book Number Four. Only a few chapters left. She just had to find out who was this ghost haunting the Lilac Inn.

Judy read the final chapters with Mouse purring in her lap.

Cleaning up her room wasn't so bad after all. She was having fun-fun-fun.

"I'm finally done," said Stink, coming into her room. "It took forever to put all my stuff *away*. So BOR-ing!"

"I'm having a blast," said Judy. "There's so much good stuff to do in my room. And I keep finding things I forgot about. My squished-penny collection. My Me Collage. Look, I even found my *happy* Magic 8 Ball."

I ATE
A

“You’re not *really* having fun cleaning your room, are you?” asked Stink.

“Magic 8 Ball,” said Judy. “Do I like cleaning my room?” Judy shook the happy-face yellow ball. She peered into the little window. “It says, *You’re 100% fun!*”

Stink looked around. “Um . . . your room looks even messier than before.”

“You could help me . . . ” said Judy.

“But—!” said Stink.

“The sooner we finish, the sooner we get to have Game Night. I mean Game *Day*.”

Stink and Judy zoomed around, putting things away in baskets, in boxes, in dresser drawers, on shelves, in closet cubbies, under the bed.

“Phew,” said Judy, plopping down on a pillow. “I’m pooped.”

“Tell me about it,” said Stink, plopping onto a pillow, too.

“Look at my room now,” said Judy. “All the junk is gone. There’s so much room, a person could turn a cartwheel in here.”

“Or karate,” said Stink. “Hi-yah!”

"Or . . ." Judy raised one eyebrow. She had an impish look on her face. She picked up her pillow and tossed it at Stink. "Pillow fight!"

Judy and Stink clobbered each other with soft, fluffy pillows.

"I'm King of the Pillows!" called Stink.

"Happy International Pillow Fight Day!" Judy climbed up to her top bunk and tossed stuffed animals at Stink. Stink used his pillow-shield to fend them off. "Ping, ping. Ping, ping, ping!" he called.

When they were all worn out, Judy and Stink collapsed on the floor in a fit of giggles.

"You were right. Cleaning up *is* fun," said Stink.

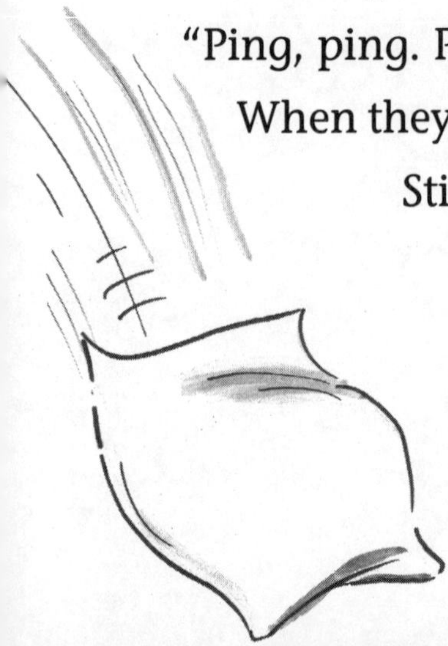

"Mom and Dad think they are so tricky getting us to clean our rooms, but they don't know how much fun we had."

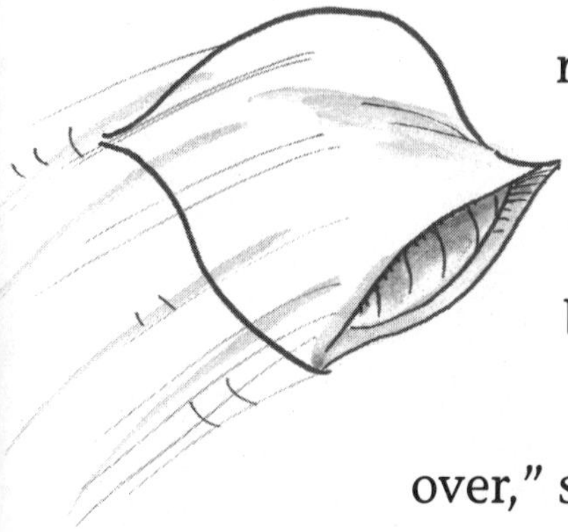

"But now we made a mess *again*," said Stink.

"Happy International Blah Blah Blah Day!" said Judy.

"And it's not even over," said Stink. "There's still Game Night. I mean Day. With popcorn!"

"Let's go wish Mom and Dad Happy National Game-Night-Day Day."

"Wait. Can a night be a day?" Stink asked.

"Why not?" said Judy. "We make the rules."

Stink grinned. "I call Mouse Trap!" said Stink. "And I get to be green."

"I call Clue!" said Judy, racing Stink down the stairs. "And I get to be Professor Plum!"

Peace Out!

Sunday. At last! Judy stayed in bed longer than usual. She curled up with Mouse and stared at the ceiling.

What a whirlwind week! She, Judy Moody, had celebrated Bubble Wrap and zucchini. She had tasted rat stew and watched a Ninja Squirrel. She had eaten ice cream for breakfast and learned how to get along with Stink. She had beaten the blahs and celebrated Blah Blah Blah Day.

She, Cats Bandicoot, had even cleaned her room and been in a pillow fight and promoted world and outer-space peace.

No wonder she felt tired. No wonder she felt like a slugabed.

Stink came in all loud mouth and spiky hair and bouncy arms and legs. "What are we going to do today? Huh? Huh? Huh?"

"It's Sunday, Stink. Day. Of. Rest."

"C'mon," said Stink. "Get out of bed, sleepyhead."

Judy sat up on her bed and began popping Bubble Wrap. Mr. Todd said popping Bubble Wrap helped with stress. She was stressed out just thinking about coming up with another holiday for today.

"Not Bubble Wrap Day again," said Stink.

"Chill out, Stinkerbell," said Judy. "I have a good idea. Today is National Do Nothing Day."

"I don't get it," said Stink. "Doing nothing isn't doing something."

"Okay, how about National Take a Nap Day?"

"Snooze fest," said Stink. He pretend-snored.

"National Read in the Bathtub Day? National Stay Home and Wear Pajamas All Day Day? National Hug Your Cat Day?"

"Boring, boring, and boring," said Stink.

"Boring sounds good to me," said Judy. "Boring sounds not-boring at all!"

"C'mon!" said Stink, yanking the covers off Judy. "We have to do something super exciting. Tomorrow is Monday."

"Monday," said Judy. "I can't wait for Monday. Plain old, boring old Monday."

"Monday? You hate Mondays! Mondays are blah. Mondays are meh. Mondays put you in a mood. Not a good mood. A bad mood."

"When a holiday comes every day, it's not so special anymore," said Judy. "Sometimes a good old Monday is all the adventure you need."

el sol

Chronicles of
NARNIA

Stink could not believe his ears. "Name one good thing about a Monday."

"It's not Thursday," said Judy.

"What else you got?" asked Stink.

Judy thought some more. "The first chocolate kiss was made on a Monday. The first book about Narnia came out on a Monday. And it rains more on all the other days of the week than on Monday."

"For reals?" asked Stink.

Judy nodded. "I read it in the *Big Head Book of Strange and Interesting Facts.*"

"Hey! That's my book," said Stink.

"If you scramble up the letters in Monday you get *dynamo*. Mighty Fantaskey told me that one. Balto, the sled dog, saved a whole town in Alaska on a

Monday. Mr. Todd taught me that one."

"But did you know that most people don't even smile until after eleven on a Monday morning?" Stink pointed out.

"I did not know that," said Judy. "We have to do something about that, Stink."

"Yes!" he said, pumping his fist in the air. "So tomorrow can be National Smile Before Eleven O'Clock Monday?"

"Sure, why not?" said Judy.

"Cool beans," said Stink. "I'm going to get my joke book and find some jokes to make you laugh first thing Monday morning."

"Good idea, Stink," said Judy.

As soon as Stink left, Judy climbed down from her top bunk. She went over

to the window and opened the curtains and pulled up the shade.

She could see the moon in the daytime. A children's moon! Judy forgot to tell Stink something else about Monday. Monday means Day of the Moon.

She, Judy Moody, could not wait for Monday! Moon Day.

Who knows? Maybe tomorrow, on an ordinary, everyday, boring old Monday, she, Judy Moody, would receive a message from outer space.

Goony al peep! We come in peace.

Surely that would make a person smile before 11:00 a.m. on the chocolate-kissed, un-moodiest, least rainy day of the week.

Goorny al peep!

Megan McDonald is the author of the popular Judy Moody and Stink series, as well as the Judy Moody and Friends series for new readers. She has written many other books for children, including the Ant and Honey Bee stories, the Sisters Club series, and several picture books. Before she began writing full-time, Megan McDonald worked as a librarian, a bookseller, and a living-history actress. She lives in Northern California with her husband, Richard Haynes, who is also a writer.

Peter H. Reynolds is the illustrator of the popular Judy Moody and Stink series in addition to many other books, including several for which he is also author. They include his Creatrilogy of picture books: *The Dot*, *Ish*, and *Sky Color*. His book *The Dot* has even inspired International Dot Day, which is celebrated around the world every September. Besides writing and illustrating, Peter H. Reynolds is a bookstore owner, animator, and educator. He lives in Massachusetts with his family.